RIGHT ON CUE

SABINE BRADLEY

An imprint of Enslow Publishing

WEST 44 BOOKS™

Please visit our website, www.west44books.com.
For a free color catalog of all our high-quality books,
call toll free 1-800-398-2504.

Cataloging-in-Publication Data

Names: Bradley, Sabine.
Title: Right on cue / Sabine Bradley.
Description: New York : West 44, 2023. | Series: West 44
YA verse
Identifiers: ISBN 9781978596160 (pbk.) | ISBN 9781978596153
(library bound) | ISBN 9781978596177 (ebook)
Subjects: LCSH: American poetry--21st century. | Poetry,
Modern--21st century. | English poetry.
Classification: LCC PS584.B733 2023 | DDC 811'.6--dc23

First Edition

Published in 2023 by
Enslow Publishing LLC
29 East 21st Street
New York, NY 10011

Editor: Caitie McAneney
Designer: Katelyn E. Reynolds

Photo Credits: Cvr, p. 1 gnepphoto/Shutterstock.com.

Printed in the United States of America

CPSIA compliance information: Batch #CS23W44: For further information contact
Enslow Publishing LLC, New York, New York at 1-800-398-2504.

*To all of my mothers,
and to my daughter.*

MOVIES ARE MOSTLY PREDICTABLE

That's what I like about them.

    A lost hero is sure to be found.
    Uncertain hearts will, over time,
let each other in.

    The storms are easy to predict.
    I can tell how things will end.
No twist I can't see coming.

I like it that way.

I'VE NEVER BEEN TO NEW YORK

I hear you could live there

      your whole life and

never see the same face twice.

I hear the city stays up

      yelling your name

from the sidewalk.

I hear every brick wall

      and park bench

is a canvas.

WORTH

I hear that's the place to go

    if you want to be

anyone worth

    remembering.

Through art.

Through some mural.

Or even film.

WHEN I'M A FILM STUDENT IN THE BIG CITY

all of my friends
will wear fuzzy berets.

All of my weekends
will be packed with invites
to art shows.
    Private parties
    with the *poshest* people.

I WILL LOOK IN THE MIRROR EVERY MORNING

And I will say to my reflection:

> Welcome to your new life.
> This is the home you have built
>
> around and for
> yourself.
>
> And you may take it with you
> anywhere.

MY FOSTER PARENTS ARE VERY MUCH IN LOVE

With each other.
With their garden.
With their friends.
And family.

And me.

They are in love
with the act of loving.

THEIR BOND

is like a time machine
bringing them back to their youth.

Sometimes I see them
dancing around the house.

Sometimes I see them
holding each other.

Frowning at some tragedy
on the news.

THEY'RE TENDER THAT WAY

Soft in their hearts
and in their smiling cheeks.

As college app season comes,
they make sure to remind me

how proud of me
        they already are.

TO *FOSTER*

means to nurture.
And they do such
a careful job.

I thank them.

And I just hope they never

change
      their minds.

I'VE BEEN A FOSTER KID

for five years
now

and everyone
knows it.

THE OTHER KIDS IN THIS TOWN ARE FINE

They skateboard or rollerblade on the
weekend.
They participate in charity
fundraisers.

Most of them know each other
or know of each other.

And to be fair,
most of them know my name.

I've been here
since middle school.

They offer a friendly wave when
they walk by.

But I can tell that none of them
really know what to say to me.

And that's okay.
I like my space.

STILL, SOME PEOPLE

like to offer up their own families
for me to borrow during the holidays.

Or whenever else they feel charitable.

They ask questions like:

> *What are you doing for*
> *Mother's Day, Alex?*
>
> *Would you like to spend*
> *Thanksgiving at my house?*
>
> *When will your foster parents*
> *finally adopt you?*

ELEPHANT IN THE ROOM

Sometimes they even ask about *HER*.
(My mother.)

When that happens, I just smile.

Mutter something about this town
being too small.

Then walk away.

HER

I never call her
by her name
or what she is
to me.

She's just HER.
Or SHE.

It's simpler
that way.

IF I HAD TO DESCRIBE HER

Picture:

A wild swan.

A yard of thorny roses.

A woman made of stained glass.

MY MOTHER HAS A BEAUTIFUL FACE

All angles and sharp edges.

    HER hair is so thick,
    I would hide in it
    as a little girl.

    I believed it was the safest
    place in the world.

In most of my memories, SHE is
    wearing a tight dress
    or leather jacket.

Twirling around. Wine-glass stem
    gripped in HER long fingers.

SHE IS A GODDESS OF LOVE

```
Able to give it
or take it away
in the time it takes

to empty a glass.
```

UNLIKE ME

SHE always had a lot of friends.

Women with too much makeup.
Men who smelled like tobacco.

SHE would introduce me to them
before dancing out the front door
for the night.

> *This is my daughter, Alex,*
> SHE would say.

> *Isn't she pretty?*
> *Doesn't she look just like me?*

Then SHE would disappear.
Into a shiny car.
Onto the back of a Harley.
Away with a shirtless lover.

When SHE got home, SHE would stink.
Of bad fruit.
Of a night spent on HER feet.

SHE would stumble into my room.
Wake me with HER cries.

I'd wrap my hands in HER hair
once again. Holding it behind HER
as SHE hurled.

I LOVE MORNINGS

I love to drink tea.
Watch the sun rise.
I sit in the wicker chair
on the back porch.

The dancing colors of the sky at dawn
make the beginning of each day
feel like the opening scene

of an adventure film.
And I am the star,

with my name spelled out
in credits
rolling in the clouds.

TIME TO GO

Mr. and Mrs. S have had the same car
    since forever.

A rusty red wagon. It moans and groans
    when the key is turned.

The seats are tan. Covered in stains.
    Burst lunch bags.
    Splashed coffee.
    Spilled nail polish.
    (From when their own daughters
    were my age.)

A thick plaid blanket in the trunk.
Just in case it gets cold and the heat
won't work.

        I know that Mr. and Mrs. S
        could afford to buy a new car.

But they swear that nothing else
would do
to transport
such special cargo.

And they never give up
on the things and people
they love.

ON THE WAY TO SCHOOL

We pass by HER house.
It's a single-floor ranch
with a single tree in the yard.

   Have you spoken to her lately?
   Mrs. S asks me.

I pause, shocked by the question.

We drive the same way to school
      every day.
      But we never bring HER up.

21

NO!

I manage to spit the word out.
My trembling voice sounds
like a sputtering engine.
I don't look up from my lap.

> *Well.*
> *Don't you want to invite her*
> *to graduation?*

I know that Mrs. S means well,
but I ignore her question.
I let it disappear
into the sound
of the red wagon's wails
as we drive on.

Besides, it's only fall.

Graduation
is months away.

I'M NOT ON ANY TEAMS

Or in any clubs.

But that's not because I'm not good
enough.

I can run as fast as anyone in school.

I've been playing chess with Mr. S
for years.

I could totally film the morning
announcements.

I just don't have the school spirit.

And honestly, I don't really
like teams.

IF THERE'S ANYONE WHO UNDERSTANDS ME

it's my art teacher,
            Ms. Owens.

She was a foster kid, too.

And she loves movies just like I do.

We both think that shark films are
      underrated.
And that musicals get way too much
      credit.

Some of the other kids say she looks
like a bird.
A flamingo or parrot.

Because she's tall. Likes to paint
her lips and eyelids
      all sorts of bright,
      beautiful colors.

But I understand Ms. Owens.
      I understand that sometimes,
      you make your art out of
      what's right in front of you.

THAT DOESN'T MEAN

I could make movies
out of my own
life.

I don't want anyone
to know
my mess.

I don't want anyone
to know
about HER.

ARE YOU EXCITED TO GO AWAY FOR COLLEGE?

Ms. Owens asks me
while we eat lunch together
in her classroom.

It's our daily ritual.

I am eating leftover casserole.
Ms. Owens is eating oatmeal.

I shrug.
I mean, sure.

> Ms. Owen tilts her oval head.
> She stirs her oats.
> *Alex, it's okay to look forward
> to things.*

I chuckle, uncomfortable
with the sudden
seriousness in her voice.

I know that,
I assure her.

Then I change the subject.

I CONSIDER MYSELF A REALIST

Of course I'm excited
when I think
of graduation.

Of course my belly somersaults
when I think of that first
important step: college.

Of course I can't wait to start
chasing my biggest dream.

But
part of the application process
is submitting a mini doc.

> That's a short documentary.
> Just five to ten minutes long.

And I've yet to even start.

I GUESS I'M ALSO A PROCRASTINATOR

I put things off.

Just as the summer began,
Mr. and Mrs. S gave me a brand-new
camera.
Not like my old one.
This one is weatherproof and expensive.

This past summer was damp.
There was a downpour almost every day.

I spent months filming the rain
as it fell on the cement.
As it filled a muddy footprint.

I just couldn't figure out
my subject.

NOW IT'S FALL

The chill in the air is hard
to show on film.

A whole season has come and gone.
And I've got a whole lot of nothing.

I hold my camera
in my gloved hands
and sigh.

FIRST IMPRESSIONS MATTER

Whatever I end up filming,
whatever I end up sending
to strangers far away—
it has to be

magical.
Hopeful.
Memorable.

There won't be a face-to-face
interview.

If I want to be accepted
to my school of choice,
I have to send them a project
that will make an impression for me.

So of course I'm excited.

      But
      I'm also terrified
      of missing the mark.

FAMILY OUTING

Mrs. S picks me up from school.
Pearl earrings peek out behind
silver wisps of hair.

Are we going somewhere?
I ask.
I know full well
what the answer must be.

Mrs. S only wears her pearls
for family outings.

> *We are.*
> *Mr. S and I thought*
> *we would go to Tizzy's*
> *for dinner tonight.*

She glances over at me as she
says this.

Tizzy's?!
I practically yell.

OUR LAST VISIT

Mrs. S keeps her eyes
on the road this time.

> *Oh Alex, I know our last visit*
> *wasn't a good one.*
>
> *But that was a while ago.*
> *Isn't it time to replace the*
> *bad memories?*

I TAKE MY TIME

getting dressed for dinner.

I am in no rush to go to Tizzy's.

It's the most popular diner in town.
The football team goes to Tizzy's
after practice.

The pastor and her family go to Tizzy's
after church.

The waitresses know everyone by name.

It's a loner's nightmare.

But there's another reason
I don't want to go.

WHEN WE ARRIVE

I swear the song playing
from behind the bar
skips a beat.

Our waitress has hot pink lipstick and
a name tag that reads "Joy."

She bounces up to us. Smiles.
Well, long time no see, family!

I cling to my frown.

Joy was working the last time we came.
I can tell from her pity
that she hasn't forgotten.

OF COURSE SHE HASN'T

forgotten the last time
we came here to meet
with HER for dinner.

Of course she's hasn't
forgotten how a public visitation
quickly turned into
a public disaster.

WHAT HAPPENED

SHE had shown up late,
tripping over herself.

SHE mumbled an apology.
Lipstick on HER teeth.

But I didn't care about any of that.
I only cared that I got to be near
HER.

I threw my arms around HER.
Pulled HER to our booth.

Ten minutes later, SHE was nodding
off.

Mom!
I pulled at HER shirt.
Mom, wake up!
People are looking at us!

HER HEAD

snapped upright.

SHE hissed through yellowing teeth.

> *Well, I'm SO sorry to*
> *embarrass you, Alex.*
> *You know, you care too much*
> *what people think.*
> *That's always been your problem.*

SHE leaned in close to my face.
Spitting the words. Holding eye
contact.

SHE pulled a travel-size bottle of
whiskey from inside HER shirt.

PROTECTIVELY

Mrs. S grabbed my wrist.
        Gentle but firm.
        She told me it was
        time to leave.

That my mother wasn't feeling well.

        That's right, Margie! SHE shouted.
        Take her away!
        Turn her against her OWN MOTHER!

Fistfuls of baked ziti flew
from HER hands.
They hit our backs as we left.

I haven't seen HER
nor the walls of this diner since.

YET HERE WE ARE

Back at Tizzy's
for the first time since the visit.

Mrs. S folds her hands and
takes a deep breath.

Your mother called today.

APPARENTLY, SHE IS SICK

And according to Mr. and Mrs. S,
it's different this time.

    It's not the kind of sickness
    that SHE could cure

    with a bowl of cheesy grits and
    a shot of bourbon whiskey.

    It's not the sickness that once
    flooded HER with such wild sadness

    that SHE lay flat,
    sobbing in the road

    until the neighbors could help me
    drag HER into our house.

No, this time it's not like that.

This sickness is not like that.
It's even meaner.

More determined.
More stubborn
than even SHE
has ever been.

THE VOICEMAIL SHE LEFT FOR ME

Hello my princess.
It's felt like forever
away from you.

I haven't been feeling well lately.
The doctors say—

well,
the doctors say I might never
feel better, baby girl.

They say
my body has grown tired
of keeping up with me.
Soon it will slow me down for good.

I know
I've left you disappointed,
time and time again.

But if you can forgive me.
Enough to come to the house
for dinner.
So I can talk to you in person.

Maybe we can figure out
how to make things right.
Together.

AT FIRST I FEEL NOTHING AT ALL

Like the first few seconds
after waking up from a strange dream.

I hardly notice my own hands
as I carefully place the phone back on
the table.

The room around me
doesn't feel quite real.

It's too foggy. Too distant.

I can no longer tell
where my feet touch the floor.

Mrs. S reaches gently for my hand.
Mr. S gives me a glass of water.

ALWAYS THE DRAMA

Why is she telling me this?
I want to know.

She's being dramatic,
right?

It's not like she's going to
        die.

Mr. and Mrs. S
look at each other.
But they don't answer me.

WHAT IS OWED

How much is lost between us
in the time we spend apart?

I come to this question over and over.
        And over
                and over.

After so many visits gone wrong,
like the last one at Tizzy's,
I stopped seeing HER altogether.

Of course I would still come across
HER in my dreams.

I'd see HER pacing outside of the
grocery store
every so often.

But I've pushed the dreams
from my mind.
I've ignored all the phone calls.
Dodged the hugs outside of the
grocery store.

Yet now,
        because of one phone call,
        I must decide how badly
        I want to hide.

WHAT IF

it's just some plan of HERS
to get me under HER thumb
yet again?

It's not difficult to imagine.
    HER, crying diseased wolf.

SHE loves to be thought of.
    SHE loves to be worried about.

How can I be sure this sickness
isn't just another way for HER
to creep back into my mind …
    and back into my life?

MONSTER

But what if
it is true?

What if all the liquor and tar
inside of HER
has turned into a horrible,
undefeatable monster?

WILL I LEAVE

my anger,
my resentments,
my memories

at the door with my shoes?

Will I find a way to smile
while wiping the fever-sweat
from HER forehead?

And even if I do,

will it heal HER?
Will it heal us?

FAIR

It's completely fair
to feel confused by this,
Mrs. S says to me.

My eyebrows shift into question marks.

But don't you think
that you owe it to yourself
to see if anything has changed?

To see what can be saved
between the two of you?

This could be a chance
to move forward
before you leave for college.

Before you look back.
And all the time is gone.

GROWING UP MEANS

making hard choices.

Growing up means
knowing at the end of the day,
    when the sun goes
        down,

and the chilled air leaves
    dew on the grass,
        you only have
            yourself to face.

I DECIDE

to take the leap of faith.

I land at HER front door.

    Or rather,
    Mr. and Mrs. S drive me there
    in their rusty red wagon.

I could walk the short distance
to HER house. But I accept
the support that Mr. and Mrs. S offer.

    You can call us at any point.
    We will come back for you
    right away, Mrs. S says.

I try to grin at them.

I chuckle dryly.
It's only one dinner.
How bad can it be?

Neither of them chuckle back.

MY FINGER BARELY TOUCHES
THE DOORBELL

I pause to breathe.

It's been about two years
since the Tizzy's incident.

Two years since
I gave up hope in HER altogether.

The wind blows a cluster
of fallen leaves around
and around.

Fears swirl inside my mind.

Will SHE mention all the missed calls?

Will SHE still smell like spoiled fruit
and dancing?

SUDDENLY

before I can muster the courage
I need to push the buzzer,

the door opens
and SHE is standing there
before me. Gushing,

Welcome home, baby!

CATCH UP

SHE leads me through the door.
The paint of the archway is
cracked and chipping.

A few loose bits tremble
and fall with our footsteps.

HER feet are dressed in furry slippers.
I don't remember ever
seeing HER wear them before.

They tap the floor softly.
As if they are kissing awake
the wooden boards
beneath the faded carpet.

FEET

When I was young
(and so was SHE),

HER feet were always arched
inside spear-like heels.

Or, they were bare.
Racing and sliding
across the floor with carelessness.
Collecting dirt under each toe.

There were no soft taps.

HURRY

SHE is out of breath already.

> *We have so much to talk about.*
> *So much to catch up on.*

SHE says this in a hurry.
As if SHE is rushing to get
the words out

> before an invisible clock with
> greedy hands
> can snatch away the chance.

PHOTOGRAPHS

clutter the walls of the living room.
They surround us now,

wrapping us in a fog
of memories.

I gaze at the pictures.
I daydream.

I travel in and out of history
as SHE asks me

question
after
question.

IT FEELS LIKE AN INTERROGATION

How is school going, baby?

Above the TV in a black wooden frame:
        a day at the beach.
        Captured in black and gray.
        HER arms circling
        around my small body.
        Both of us beaming toward
        the camera.

Do you have a boyfriend?

Taped to the wall near the hallway:
        a Christmas tree glowing.
        Decorated with red and
        gold ornaments.
        Popcorn strung together
        on twine.

*When did your hair get
so long?*

WALKING ON ICE

It's a strange feeling.
    A strange way to spend an
    evening.

    Tiptoeing over the thin ice that
    separates us from each other.

I'm so afraid that I will slip.
    Will lose balance while skating
    across this delicate ground.

There is so much
that could break.
So much that could be shattered
by what we say next.

So, is it true? Are you sick?
I ask HER.

SHE CLOSES HER EYES

Exhales slowly.

> *I think, in some ways,*
> *I've been sick for a*
> *very*
> *long*
> *time.*

THE FIRST SUPPER

SHE asks if I've eaten
      and I say no.

SHE suggests that we cook dinner
together.

Partly because it is getting close to
dinnertime
and partly because,
as we all know,
food is the key
that unlocks all mouths.

JUST LIKE THAT

Broken hearts come together
to set the table.

An angry soul cools itself
to make room for a hot meal.

LIKE A DANCE WE NEVER FORGOT

SHE pulls meat from the refrigerator.
Dumps it into a large mixing bowl.
Points me to the spices.

I pull seasoning from splintering
wooden shelves.

Salt and pepper: a solid foundation.
Cayenne: for heat.
Cinnamon: to quiet the cayenne when it
is too loud.

SHE slides the bowl of bleeding,
raw beef
toward me on the counter.

I add the spices.
Plunge my hands into the mixture.

The meat is cold. Icy crystals
in the blood.

I squeeze and turn it over
in my fingers.

Trying not to spill blood
over the unusual quiet
that fills my childhood home.

EVERYTHING SEEMS DIFFERENT

The baggy wool sweater
SHE is wearing today.

Very different from the
shiny black leather
SHE wore to my sixth-grade graduation.

The throw pillows resting
on the couch tonight.

Very different from the grimy men or
cackling women
who used to lounge on its cushions.

HER eyes are different—
                    less wild.

HER walk is different—
                    less tiger.

SHE picks up a glass and fills it
     with water.

WE EAT OUR MEAL IN SILENCE

And then it's time for me to leave.
SHE asks when I will visit again.

It becomes clear through HER eager
face that our roles are reversed.

For the first time all evening,
I notice that I'm taller than HER now.

Now, it is SHE looking up at me,
with wide eyes.

Now it is SHE who will be waiting
by the window for me.

NOW IT IS I

who must choose
if and when

I will walk back
through the front door.

A MOTHER IS A MOTHER

No matter the disease.

No matter the words spoken.
How harsh they bite.
How loudly they ring.

A mother is
always a mother.

Even when she is a ghost.

A MOTHER IS PERSISTENT

and hopeful.

I try to focus on schoolwork, on film.
But every afternoon, right on cue,
SHE calls.

I tell Mrs. S to take a message.

SHE leaves voicemails day after day.
Like the soundtrack to a sad and cliché
movie.

I listen to them.
I bask in them.

        But I do not call HER back.

I WANT TO TAKE MY TIME

I want to find my footing.

I want to savor our first decent time
spent together in years.

Like a sweet dessert after
a bitter main course.

And so I do not call HER back
for three whole weeks.

I KNOW IT ISN'T RIGHT

But the truth is,
I am actually enjoying this.

The odd sense of power.
Of justice.

Of knowing that SHE
is so hungry for my time.

REPLAY

But when it gets late,
and Mr. and Mrs. S have gone to bed,
I sneak downstairs.

I replay HER voicemails.

I sit like a flannel pajama pretzel.
I clutch the phone with both hands.

Press it to my ear until it hurts.

IT'S IRONIC

The sweet sound
of HER voice calling for *me*
for once.

It fills me with a
smug peace.

I sway back and forth
to the lullaby.

ONLY WHEN I THINK I'VE MADE HER WAIT LONG ENOUGH

do I reach out.
　　　But not a day sooner.

HER voice is almost frantic.
SHE is bursting with questions.

>　　*Alex!*
>　　*Oh, I'm so glad you called.*
>
>　　*I was afraid that you didn't*
>　　*enjoy our last visit.*
>　　*I was afraid that I did*
>　　*something wrong.*
>
>　　*You did enjoy our last visit,*
>　　*didn't you?*
>　　*I didn't do anything wrong,*
>　　*did I?*
>
>　　*Was the meatloaf overcooked?*
>　　*Do you even still like meatloaf?*
>
>　　*Why haven't you answered?*
>　　*When are you coming back?*

STILL LIFE

At school, Ms. Owens shows us
examples of still life paintings.

She says that the goal of still life
is to capture
the deeper meaning behind
simple things.

We each choose an item.
One that appears meaningless.

We're supposed to create that object
and bring meaning to it on paper.

I begin to sketch the recycling bin on
the sidewalk in front of HER house.

Then, I make a split-second decision
to do something I've never done.

I draw HER, small and blurry,
standing on the porch in the
background.

> Ms. Owens smiles,
> looking over my shoulder.
> *Wonderful details, Alex.*

MIDDLE OF OCTOBER

The ground becomes crisp.

SHE calls, yet again.

SHE needs help raking her yard.

SHE is far too lightheaded
and cannot do it herself.

I FIND THIS ODD

SHE has never cared much
for keeping a neat yard.

I can't remember a summer
when the grass in front of HER house
didn't offend the neighbors.

I can't remember an autumn
when the path to HER front steps wasn't
hidden by sheets of red and orange
leaves.

Despite this observation,
I agree to help after school
the next day.

SHE IS PERCHED ON THE STOOP

Waiting for me when I arrive that
afternoon.

Waiting to spot me as I turn
the corner.
Like a mountain lioness

on the hunt for a second chance.
Hoping to grasp forgiveness between
HER paws.

HER teeth gleam in the golden
October light.

SHE STARES AT ME

as I gather leaves,
dragging them into a
large pile.

I can feel HER eyes on me.
They follow every footstep
across the yard.

You know,
you don't have to wait for me out here,
I call out.

I'm annoyed by HER staring.

You can go inside. I'll let you know
when I'm done.

SHE lowers her gaze,
and stutters a bit.

OH

Oh, okay.
Right.

Well, tell you what,
why don't I go make us some
hot chocolate?

You do like hot chocolate,
don't you?

Then SHE finally
leaves me alone.

THE SMELL OF WARM MILK

floats through the air.
Fills my nose as I walk
through the screen door.

I'm finished with the yard.
The leaves are bagged
and by the road.

I peer into the kitchen.

SHE is pouring steaming hot chocolate
into a pair of matching mugs.

> *That's nice.*
> SHE replies absently.
>
> *I mean, thank you.*
> *Marshmallows or no marshmallows?*

SHE IS DETERMINED

to keep me stuck to the couch
with creamy peanut butter
spread across soft cookies

and endless
refills of warm, rich cocoa.

ENOUGH

But I came to help a sick woman with
her yard.
That's all.

Eventually
I stand. Stretch my legs.

I say to HER:
I've had enough to eat.

SHE frowns toward the setting sun.
HER disappointed face is lit up
by its colors.

NEVER-ENDING TASKS

It becomes a pattern,
a montage speeding past,
      in the sepia tones of fall.

I go to school. Spend lunch with Ms.
Owens.
Head home to do homework.

But there is always a voicemail.
Always a message from HER.

There is always a request, a task
that HER ailing body cannot do.

There is always something that SHE
desperately needs
      from me.

I'M AWARE

yet unable
to resist.

I put everything aside
and continue

to come to
HER rescue.

WHAT'S NEXT

After the leaves, it's a maze of bins
and boxes
scattered around HER basement.

After the basement, it's three black
trash bags
full of dirty laundry.

After the laundry, it's dried scum and
matted hair
clinging to the bathtub.

ANNOYED

My fingers clench tightly
as I scrub the sides of the tub.

I can faintly hear HER singing,
over the sound of steel wool
scratching against the worn ceramic.

I scowl, my ears warm.
I scrub harder as her voice
travels down the hall.

I SNAP

Tub's clean,
I huff through
pursed lips.

The corners of her mouth pull into a
too-sweet grin. My stomach turns.

> *Perfect timing.*
> *Grilled cheese on the stove.*

No thanks.
I plunge my arms
into the sleeves of my coat.

I'm leaving. Unless
you have more chores for me,
that is.

A LOOK OF UNDERSTANDING

washes over HER face.
HER head tilts in thought.
SHE sighs a soft apology.
SHE appears even shorter than before.

> *Of course not, my love.*
> *You have been so helpful.*

TIRED AND UNTRUSTING

I walk back to Mr. and Mrs. S's house
in a foul mood.

I feel used and foolish.

She's at it again!
I shout as I arrive home.
I kick my shoes off of my feet.
They hit a wall.

My heels and toes ache.
Raw from stomping home.

>   *What was that, Alex?*
>   *Who's at what now?*
>   Mrs. S calls out
>   from the back porch.

I RANT

Her self-centered mind games!

    I answer.
    My suspicion spills
    out of my mouth.

She calls us up,
says she's dying or whatever.

And BOOM! Just like that.
she has a personal maid, landscaper,
and audience.

What more could she want?

DEVIL'S ADVOCATE

Alex, your mother is ill.
It makes sense for her to need
some extra help
around the house.

I shake my head, impatient.
I have no energy to humor Mrs. S.
Or to match her endless compassion.

MRS. S CONTINUES

Is it possible,
that all of that housework
is just a way for her
to spend time with you?

Your mother is desperate
to make things right.
I've spoken with her about it
over the phone.
Quite a few times.

Every single time
that she has called
looking for you.

SOON

You know, soon she will have
twelve entire months sober
under her belt.

Wouldn't be the first time,
I reply. I roll my eyes
at the popcorn ceiling.

I am tired and unimpressed
with the announcement.

I am, after all, a realist.

IT ISN'T MY AIM TO BE COLD

But years spent away from HER have not
made me forget the frigid truth.

If sobriety is a hopeful summer,
then it's safe to say that winter
is always around the corner.

SHE is only as constant
        as the fickle seasons.

And I learned long ago
        that you can't trust the weather.

ALL HALLOWS' EVE

I spend Halloween indoors.

Watching old horror films with
Mr. and Mrs. S.

Listening for the mischievous laughter
of trick-or-treaters.

We spend the spooky holiday
together this way
every year.

THE TELEVISION RUMBLES

as growling monsters crawl
across the screen.

I can feel Mrs. S jump in place
next to me on the couch.

I laugh at her, and she smiles.
This feels so perfectly *normal*.

AND THEN

Ding dong.

The bell rings.

It's my turn
to answer the door.

I carry a bowl
full of sugary candies.

Taffy and
        caramels.

Licorice and
        bubble gum.

A TREAT

Trick or treat!
shouts a small
but passionate voice.

A little girl stands in the doorway.
A patch covers one eye.
A toy parrot sits atop her shoulder.
A brown hat is tilted on her head.

I'm the pirate queen of the high seas!
        She lifts her eyepatch
        to search for tasty treasure.

She grabs a fistful of sweets.
Then she turns.
Skips into the waiting arms of a woman
wearing gray sweatpants.

                What do you say?
                the woman prompts.

The girl tips her hat's brim toward us.
Thank you!

Mr. S and I smile and wave. The little
pirate pulls at the woman's sweatpants.

C'mon, Mom!
Let's do the next house now!

MY HEART BREAKS

for the child
within me

who never got
a mother-daughter

moment
like that.

WE SETTLE BACK IN TO WATCH THE MOVIE

Just a few minutes
and some jump scares later,
    we hear the doorbell again.

Mr. S and I rise from the couch
together,
both expecting to see another pair
    of small, outstretched hands.

A TRICK

Instead,
we see HER standing outside.

Staring at the incoming clouds.
Tapping on a dusty broomstick.
Letting it wobble between HER fingers.

>*Oh!*
>*Happy Halloween.*
>SHE says, bringing HER gaze
>back down to earth suddenly.

As if SHE had forgotten
where SHE was for a moment.

SHE HOVERS IN THE DOORWAY

HER eyes
     dart gently. Subtly
       but surely.

From my unimpressed scowl
     to Mr. S and his raised brows.

Then further into the house,
     toward the living room.

Mrs. S patiently waits,
the TV remote by her side.

DISGUISES

A simple black bag hangs from HER
shoulder.
SHE reaches inside and pulls out a
pointy,
plastic nose.

> *It's a witch's nose.*
> SHE explains the obvious,
> though I did not ask.

How fitting.
I reply. I roll my eyes.

Then turn my back to HER.

THE SKIN ON MY BACK

can sense HER closeness.

SHE follows me inside.

HER footsteps fall only inches
behind my own.
I quicken my pace. Trying my best
to create a larger gap between us.

I feel HER fingers graze my arm.
Irritation *zings* through every muscle.

I whip my head toward HER.

WHAT?!

THE HUMAN TONGUE

has eight flexible muscles.

All eight can transform from soft
tissue
    to the sharpest steel.

    From soft flesh
    to a fatal sword

    at a moment's notice.

WORDS THAT HURT

HER eyes grow wide. Then they shimmer
with the dewy film of held-back tears.

> SHE stammers:
> *I just wanted us to go*
> *trick-or-treating together.*
> *We never got the chance to*
> *when you were small.*

I LET OUT A GRUNT

My disbelief is caught in my throat.

W—we didn't get the chance?
I'm sure it's easier to say it that
way.
But really!?

I shake my head and snicker.
My body boils with bitterness.

No, Mom.
No, we had plenty of chances.
You just chose to waste them all.

THE ROOM GETS HOTTER AND HOTTER

Spite broils inside of my mouth.
It reaches the brim of my lips.

You don't always get to be the victim!
I announce, righteously.

You don't get to fly in on your broomstick
and magically make the worst half
of my life disappear!

It doesn't work that way.
No matter how sick you claim to be.
No matter how wet with booze your brain is!

MY FAULT?

Alex!
Mrs. S scolds me.

She gestures disapprovingly
toward my mother's pained expression.

But it doesn't make me
feel bad.

It just makes me
angrier.

HER TEARS

can no longer
be stopped from falling
from HER dry, tired face.

They discolor
HER cheeks,
leaving behind thin,
pale streaks.

HER eyes are wet and shiny,
streams of saltwater
melting HER coffee-cake complexion.

SUDDENLY SHE STOPS

And SHE lets out a faint groan.
HER knees tremble.

First only a little.
Then wildly.

Then they give out completely.
I assume they're buckling under
the crushing weight of guilt.

WHEN THE PARAMEDICS ARRIVE TO TAKE MY MOTHER

Mr. and Mrs. S start the car
so we can follow behind HER.

I can only barely
see through smudges on
the ambulance's tiny back window.

But still, I squint and strain.
I need to keep HER
in my sight.

I TELL MYSELF

to think logically
as I sit in one of the many stiff chairs
that fill the hospital waiting room.

The paisley fabric of the seat smells
of dust and rubbing alcohol.

I tell myself that SHE has taken many
trips to emergency rooms before.

After tumbling down a staircase.
Forgetting to drink water for
too many days in a row.

I REMIND MYSELF

that I am a realist.
That I should be realistic.
That the things I said to HER
are in no way responsible

for the haunting *thud*
of HER forehead hitting the hardwood.

That is what I tell myself.

BUT I CAN'T HELP FEELING

```
like maybe it was
the thunder of rejection
that shook HER.
```

A FEW HOURS PASS

Finally, a doctor approaches us.
Suggests we go home for tonight.
Promises us SHE will be okay.

SHE needs rest.

My heart reaches for that promise
and holds it tight.

As we exit the hospital,
an owl screeches into the
Halloween sky.

MY SHAME

surrounds me in my bed.
Like an itchy wool
blanket.

It covers my skin in hives.
Makes me sweat.

My stomach rolls inside my body.

I CANNOT FIND PEACE

So I write
all of my anxieties
into a flimsy notepad.

Hoping to find the words
to lull me to sleep.

LOVE IS A RICKETY SEESAW

The creaking wood of a
roller coaster's old tracks.
A fickle fuse.
A lamp flickering through the night.

There is no kind of love that does not
leave you wondering
where the broken wheel is.
And how long it will be

until everything falls apart.
Perfection is a myth.
And perfect love is a kingdom of
empty castles.

My mother's blood runs through me.
It fills my spirit so that
I will always love her.

Regardless of all
our combined faults.

Love her in ways that surprise
everyone.

In ways that surprise
me, most of all.

THERE'S A SHIFT IN ME

Now when I think of her,
I don't want to separate her
from myself.

I want her with me,
always.

I just want my mother
to live.

THE EYES

are the trickiest body parts to tame.
They are honest and wild by nature.

Even the best actors struggle to keep
their true selves
hidden behind those tell-all windows
to the soul.

WHEN I ENTER MY MOTHER'S HOSPITAL ROOM

our eyes meet,
brought together by that
invisible string
between mother and child
that never fully disappears.

Her green-brown eyes search my own.

We each release streams of
silent tears.

TEARS CARRY MESSAGES THAT ONLY WE CAN HEAR

I am sorry.

*I've forgotten the way to
the place where love lives.*

*I've left my pain behind,
so I may make it to you quicker.*

I love you.

I've always loved you.

I'm sorry.

Forgive me.

HOW ARE YOU FEELING?

I finally find the courage
to ask out loud.

> She struggles to sit up
> under the paper-thin sheets.
>
> Her reply is simple:
> *I feel bad.*

I cross the shiny waxed floor
and go to her side.
Without thinking.
Without a second's pause.

It feels so natural
to love her again.

We fall into each other's arms
on the hospital bed.

LIKE SO MANY TIMES BEFORE

I find that I am rushing to her.

    Much like someone would rush to
    smother a fire.
    As if my embrace could stop
    the burning, crumbling
    pieces inside her.

Like so many times before,
    I forget myself.

Forget my raw and bitter wounds.
I'm taken over by animal compassion.
The overpowering instinct of a
child's never-ending love.

Like so many times before,

    I stroke her forehead with the
    back of my hand.

    Tuck her in as if I am putting
    my younger self to bed.

    And whisper to us both:
It will be better in the morning.

THE PLAZA OFF THE EASTBOUND HIGHWAY

has the oldest cluster of storefronts
in the city.
They're already decorating for
Christmas.

At the entrance to the parking lot,
there's a large, decorative archway.
Painted blue metal.

I have passed this archway more times
than I can count.

Counting on the three balloons on top
of the arch: red, yellow, blue.

I know with certainty I will see them
dancing whenever I visit the plaza.

No matter what happens.

BUT SOMETHING'S CHANGED

On our drive home from the hospital,
we pass the familiar plaza.

For the first time,
I look up toward the gate, and see
stiff iron balloons, rusting
on the archway.

When did that happen?
I ask no one in particular.

      But inside I know that nothing
      has changed.
      Only my youthful vision.

MY MOTHER STRUTS

out of the hospital a few days later.
Strides long. Head high.
As if to boast, to spit
in the face of any petty illness.

She hasn't driven a car or
had her license in years.

So Mr. S and I wait
for her nearby,
the red wagon parked
at the curbside.

For a moment,
I am impressed.

In this moment,
she seems so untouched
by sickness or time.

She seems, like every mother
does to her child,

invincible
and immortal.

PROS AND CONS

No one can possibly be
ALL good.

A perfect character isn't likeable.
Any good filmmaker understands this.

Every hero has a flaw.
Every protagonist has something
to learn.

THE TRUTH IS

my mother is as complex
as the avant-garde paintings
we study in Ms. Owens's art class.

She is a colorful pool of depth.
She is a crooked and cracked frame.

She is a masterpiece whose canvas
is stained where a nearby glass
spilled

and left its mark on
a beautiful image.

WE FALL INTO A ROUTINE

After school,
I run to my mother's house.

We fill ourselves until we are
bloated and bursting with warm
food and memories.

We do this
at least
three times a week.

Fear and hunger offer us common ground
on which to dine together.

And we slowly

        slowly

plant seeds that resemble forgiveness.

A NEW NORMAL

The strangest thing
about this new normal

is the many ways in which
it mimics our old chaos.

Mom loses her balance often,
though now it happens
without a cocktail.

She no longer sleeps in, but
her eyelids begin to fall after
only a short time out of bed.

I don't mind helping her stumble
down the hallway anymore.

And I fear that is because
    some part of me
knows I won't always have the chance.

MY MOTHER NEVER WENT TO COLLEGE

She barely graduated high school.
I ask why, and she squints in thought.

>   *Just never cared for classrooms,*
>   she says.

I tell her that I am applying for
college
in New York City.

She beams like the sun
looking proudly upon a sprout.

She tells me
that I am going to bloom
in a city
like that.

WHAT MAY COME

My mother never went to college.

    But she has seen so much
    of the world.

I imagine her at my age:

    Fingers tracing
    an outstretched map.

Head resting against the window
of a randomly chosen train.

    Her grin full of adventure.

My mother never went to college.

    But I imagine her at my age.

Heart open wide.
Ready to embrace
what may come.

AND I KNOW

that this too
is a sort of legacy
worth
keeping
alive.

A NEW HOME FOR WINTER

It's the weekend.
The morning air is wet and cold.

But the sun is high and its rays
stretch across the yard like golden
streamers.

I drape a blanket over my shoulders.
Warm my hands with a mug of hot tea.

I look toward the back deck and see
Mrs. S repotting her favorite plants
to bring inside for winter.

Mrs. S smiles as I join her.

We chat and chuckle
and get dirt under our fingernails.

ANOTHER MOTHER

I love Mrs. S,
and she loves me.

I pat the soil around the roots
of a sage cutting.

I hope you know,
I say, in a serious tone.

No matter how much time
I spend with my mother these days,

I still love you.
I'm still so grateful to be part of
this family.

Mrs. S tilts her head and grins.
She touches my cheek and says,

> *If there's anything*
> *this old bird knows,*
> *it's that there is always*
> *enough love*
> *to share.*

AFTER THANKSGIVING

Ms. Owens asks me if I need any help
with my documentary submission.

She says she would love to see
what I have so far.
Offer any advice.

The deadline is only a month
or so away.

I think she can tell
I've been horribly distracted.

*I'm still trying to find the right
subject,*
I say. My heart sinks.

I've only filmed bits
here and there,
nothing that I want
to share.

> *You only have until January,*
> Ms. Owens cautions.

DANCING IN THE FOG

I'm visiting my mother
one early December evening.

We spend hours sitting together
by the front door.
Watching as the raindrops fall
in perfect rhythm.

It pours in an almost-shy mist.
The air is cool and satisfying.

A calm before winter.

We stay silent, my mom and I,
both staring into the moist fog.

The light tapping of the soft rain
on the ground echoes warmly.

> *It almost sounds like music,*
> *don't you think?* she asks.

AND THEN MY MOTHER

reaches for my hand,
laces HER long fingers into mine.
Pulls me from the doorway
into the misty rain.

It isn't raining hard enough
to soak our clothes or hair.

But the fog lends a smoke effect.
Framing our bodies as we spin.

I think about how great it'd be
to capture this moment together
on film.

In this moment, though,
        I worry about nothing but
        where my dancing feet will land.

ON THE GOOD DAYS

you would never guess
there is anything wrong.

Mom smiles often,
stretches out in blue jeans
like she hasn't a care in the world.

On those days, we read gossip columns.
Gush over dreamy Hollywood stars
on magazine covers.

We do each other's makeup.
She tells me about her first love.

(His name was Kevin.
After they split up,
she was never kissed
the same way again.)

She asks me questions about
film and directing.
I show her how my camera works.

BUT SOME DAYS ARE BAD

She stares blankly into space.
Unable to move her throbbing body
without wincing.

On the bad days, we skip dinner
because she can't keep her food down.

On the bad days, I try not to let her
see me cry. But she does.
And she says,

> *It's okay, lovebug, you can cry.*
> *Today is a good day for crying.*

And so we both cry.

ARE YOU AFRAID?

I ask my mother one afternoon.
We rock together on the porch swing.

> *Afraid? Of what? Dying?*
> *No. Now, don't get me wrong,*
> *I don't want to die.*
> *But I'm not afraid.*

I lay my head on her lap.
I watch the clouds float past.

You are very brave.

WHAT I DON'T SAY IS THAT I AM AFRAID

I am not brave like my mother.

I have her dark, green-brown eyes.
I have her thick brows.
I have her laugh and her bee allergy.

But I do not have her fearlessness.

I wish that I could shrug coolly
in the face of things as big as
life and death.

But
I have not learned how.

And if I lose her now, then
who will teach me?

WHEN THE BAD DAYS TURN INTO NIGHT

I find it hard to sleep.
I worry and imagine Mom tripping
on the uneven floors in her home.
At school I float through the halls.

I barely feel my body, except for my
heavy eyelids.

Ms. Owens notices.

> *Alex, you fell asleep,*
> she says after class.

I struggle to look up at her,
both embarrassed and exhausted.

I'm so sorry, Ms. Owens.
I just haven't gotten much sleep
the past few days.

> Ms. Owens's voice is serious
> but concerned.
> *I know there is a lot of*
> *intense change*
> *going on for you right now.*
>
> *It's important that you*
> *take care of yourself*
> *enough to keep up.*

I nod and promise to do better.

A NEW KIND OF CHRISTMAS

Mom is feeling strong
on Christmas Eve.

So she comes to
Mr. and Mrs. S's house.

The four of us all
make dinner together.

I'm a little embarrassed
by how happy I am.

To just spend time with this
patchwork family of mine.

A PERFECT MOMENT

Mr. S chortles at his own joke.
He carelessly mixes a salad,
turning the bowl faster and faster
as he laughs.

A piece of romaine is flung into his
gray beard.
Mrs. S plucks it out lovingly.

Mrs. S and my mother set the
table together.
My plate is placed
between theirs.

I reach into my book bag
and pull out my camera.

The red recording dot flashes.

I stand back and
smile wide.

The whole frame is love.

WHEN DINNER IS ALMOST OVER

Mom makes an announcement:

Next week marks
my twelfth month sober.

It isn't that impressive,
I know. But I'm proud.

There is a celebration
at my support group

for friends and family.
I want you all to know

that you being there would
mean the world to me.

MY MOTHER'S 12-STEP GROUP

meets every Wednesday
in a church basement with
pastel green wallpaper.

She tells me about the people
she meets there
even though that's
against the rules.

There's a surgeon who gets high
to get through her 60-hour shifts.

There's an old man with a gold
tooth who lost the real one in a
bar fight.

There's a woman with a family
that doesn't know how bad her
drinking is.

The surgeon tells the best jokes.

The old man always compliments
everyone in the room.

The secret-keeper knits scarves for
the whole group.

My mother talks of them fondly.

And I am her partner in crime—
happy to listen.

ROSE-COLORED GLASSES

Before we get to her 12-month
sobriety celebration,
we stop by the local florist
and I get her a rose.

In the church basement,
a candle fills the
room with the scent of warm nutmeg.

There are foldable gray chairs
lined in rows for friends and
family.

I scan the group until I see my
mother.
I bounce up to her and open myself
up
for a hug.

She leans in quickly and faintly
returns the embrace with one arm.

Mr. and Mrs. S find four empty
seats.
I rest my head on my mother's
shoulder.
She doesn't look at me.

And I don't overthink it.

GIVING THANKS

The group members take turns
recounting their stories.
Giving thanks for the ups and downs
that brought them here.

When it's Mom's turn to speak,
she smiles uncomfortably.

She looks at the pepper-colored
carpet. The man with the gold tooth
calls out:
Don't be shy! We're all family here!

She blinks once, then chuckles.
And as if a switch has been flipped,
she once again seems like
her old charming self.

IT'S A SHORT SPEECH

She fills a few minutes with buzzwords
like:

    amends

    faith

    hope

She thanks the group.
Then lowers herself back into her
chair.

Are you feeling alright, Mom?
I whisper to her
as the next member begins to share.

    I'm fine,
    she assures me,
    placing her hand over mine.

She turns her attention
toward the speaker.

AFTER THE CELEBRATION

Mom calls less and I try
not to notice.

Our afternoons together get less
and less
frequent.

The dinner table gets quieter
and quieter
with each visit.

I choose to believe that
it's nothing.

Mom is ill.
She's tired and needs rest.

I choose not to worry so much.

I CHOOSE NOT TO WORRY

even when she stops gossiping with me
about the people in her group.

I choose not to worry even when she
stops accepting rides from
Mr. and Mrs. S
to her doctor's appointments.

I choose not to worry even when she
begins to rush our visits along.
Seeming impatient.

Let's get you home before dark.

I choose not to worry.
But I do notice.

TIME

Time will sneak past you.

Time will strike when you
aren't looking.

Time will pickpocket your plans.

OUT OF TIME

I drag through the school hallways.

I let my head fall and rest
against my locker.
Two of my schoolmates chat
a few feet away.

Sam says,
I'm so glad to just be done.
All the endless forms and paperwork.

Avery nods in agreement.
Honestly, I didn't think I would
make the deadline.

My heart drops to my stomach.
The deadline.

I reach for my phone to check the
date.
January 15th.

The final day to submit to my
dream school has arrived.
And I couldn't be less prepared.

I only have snippets of video,
and nothing edited.

I run, panicked, to Ms. Owens's room.
She's at her desk grading papers.

It's over.

I forgot all about the
application deadline.
I thought I'd have more time.

Ms. Owens drops her grading pen.
She looks at me sadly.

   Oh, Alex.

LATE AGAIN

My mother and I had planned to see
each other again
for dinner that night.

She says that she has an appointment
and will be home late.

So I wait for her on the front porch
with my camera in my hand.

My tears freeze on my face,
knowing I just blew my chances
at film school.

I film the bustling traffic
and the crows in the blue sky.

As if that'll make a difference
now.

AFTER A WHILE

the air becomes colder.

I pull my coat closer.

The sky turns from blue
to pink
to black.

But I keep waiting.

My stomach rumbles and
my eyelids get heavy.

But I keep waiting.

I WAIT

I wait until the streetlights turn on.
I wait until Mr. and Mrs. S begin to
worry.
I wait until they drive over to find
me.

And then I wait for an explanation.
I wait right next to the phone.

Thinking,
This is your cue, Mom.

I stay awake waiting.

FOR DAYS, THEN WEEKS

I wait until I have left so many
voicemails that her phone's mailbox
won't take any more messages.

I mourn film school.

But worse,
I miss my mom.

NON-CANONICAL

In the world of TV and movie fandom,
if something is "canon," that means that
it's a real, confirmed
part of the story.

However,
if something is "non-canonical,"
it's just fanfiction.

Any version of this story
where my mother
is healed, inside and out,

any version of this story where she
becomes the mother that I dream up
when I am feeling hopeful,

is non-canonical.

Something I made up.

The real story does not end that way.

A PREVIEW TO HEARTBREAK

I dream that she and I are
walking carelessly
down the side of a long
and bending river.

Our feet are bare and our toenails
are painted the same
shade of lavender.

We giggle and lean on each other
like best friends.
Try not to slip on the
algae-covered rocks.

My mother lets go of my hand.
I squeeze, trying to keep my grip.

She slides out of my grasp
with such softness
that I'm not sure if I ever
really held her at all.

The twilight sky sends light dancing
down her striking face.

For a moment I am so entranced by my
mother's effortless beauty that I do
not notice her skipping closer

and closer

to the edge of a waterfall
down the river.

THE WIND PICKS UP SPEED

until it is roaring in my ear.
I see her mouth three words:

I love you.

Then she stretches her arms out
and falls down the cliff.

THE NIGHT MY MOTHER DIES

I have nightmares and cold sweats.

I toss and turn for hours,
        stuck in the restless
limbo between
        sleep and wakefulness.

I jostle around in my bed.
Try to drift back into
troubled slumber.

Then I feel a hand on my back.

Gentle—
        but urgent.

It shakes me alert.

Mrs. S is sitting at the
foot of my bed.
Her eyes
wide.

Has she been crying?
She never cries.

What's going on?
I ask.

WHAT'S GOING ON

The hospital called Mrs. S
     just minutes past midnight.

It turns out, my mother has asked
that Mrs. S be put down as her
emergency contact.

Slowly, my sleepless mind
     begins to piece it together.

The hospital called?
What's the emergency?

I TWIST MY ANKLE

the night my mother dies.

I leap from the rusty door
of the old red wagon.

I hurry through the hospital's
parking garage.

I don't tell my body to run,
but it does.

And before I know it
Mr. and Mrs. S are yards
and yards behind me.

I frantically climb a staircase.

I look down at my feet,
sneakers blurring as they
alternate strides.

Mr. S calls for me to
Wait up!

And I do try to wait.
But my legs
do not obey.

I can only keep running.

THE WAITING ROOM FEELS LIKE A SAUNA

the night my mother dies.

Despite the fact that it is winter
and there is frost on the windows.

Anxiety makes my chest tight
and covers my forehead
with beads of sweat.

FINALLY

a very tall man in a white coat walks
in.
He looks at a clipboard.

I'm looking for the family of
Marie Giles.

The sound of my mother's name
sends my body
into electric urgency
once again.

I KNOCK MY CHAIR BACK AS I STAND

I yell too loudly,
Yes?!

The tall doctor makes a face.
Like he is both
embarrassed
and deeply sorry for me.

Then he motions for us
to follow him down the
hallway.

I'M PARALYZED

the night my mother dies.

I stand
motionless
     in the doorway
     that leads to her room.

A HOSPITAL IS FULL OF SOUNDS

The rattling of gurneys being pushed.
The constant beeping of the monitors.
The loud cries of friends and family.

Sometimes in joyous relief.

Sometimes in grief.

A hospital is full of sounds.
But they all quickly fade until

they are nothing
but a faint buzz in the background.

My ears zero in
on the sound
of her slow,
stuttering breath.

I'm here, Mom.

I FORCE MYSELF TO REALLY LOOK AT HER

the night my mother dies.

Her eyes are bloodshot and
popping forward.
Her skin is a grayish yellow.
Her lips are cracked and brittle.

Where have you been?
What were you doing?
Where did you go?

I have so many questions to ask her
about the last few weeks.

And I don't think I'll ever
know the answers.

All I can do is memorize her face.

I don't want to remember her this way.

IN THIS MOMENT

I realize that
the most important kind of love
is the kind that sees you.

The kind that loves you deep enough
to bear witness to all of your horrible
truths
and still refuses to look away.

She deserves this love.
We both do.

IT HAPPENS TOO QUICKLY

One moment,
I am resting
my cheek on her cheek.

The next moment,
her chest rises and falls.
Then does not rise again.

FAST MOTION

When Mrs. S watches sad movies,
she always fast-forwards past the
sad parts.

What's the point of watching it at all?
I always tease her.

In the weeks after my mother dies,
it's as if my brain tries to
fast-forward
through the grief.

Her funeral is a blur that I feel
both guilty and lucky
to forget.

NORMAL

Mr. and Mrs. S insist that
I talk to a grief counselor.

Her name is Dr. Jean-Pierre.
She's obsessed with telling me
how perfectly normal everything is.

I haven't cried
yet,
I say.

>   *That's normal,*
>   she replies.

I hate her for
dying,
I confess.

>   *That's normal,*
>   she assures.

I hate myself
for not being
enough to save
her,
I sob.

>   *That feeling is completely*
>   *normal,*
>   she promises.

IT'S MADDENING

Because my concern is not
whether my grief is normal.

My concern is
whether it will ever end.

MY MOTHER'S DEATH TIES MY TONGUE

Nobody likes to admit that dead people
once were living. And therefore,
once were horribly flawed
just like the rest of us.

I say this during a session with
Dr. Jean-Pierre.

I tell her that talking
about my childhood
feels sinful now.

Saying that she was anything
but perfect
feels like speaking ill of the dead.

> *But isn't it far worse*
> *to recast your mother*
> *with a fantasy version*
> *of herself?*
> Dr. Jean-Pierre asks me.
>
> *Remember her as she was.*

CHARACTER PROFILE

Dr. Jean-Pierre is right.

What good is a love that is
not honest?
What good is a love that does not love
the whole of you?

So during our next session,
I let my love expand.

I recall my mother
in all her chaotic glory.

MARIE GILES

Born on the first day of summer,
she burst into this world full of
soul.

Always the wayward child.
Always the rebel with her own cause.

She drank too much.
She smoked too much.

She never could help me
with my math homework.

In fact, she couldn't even
do long division.

But when I was six
and ran into a thicket of toxic
hogweed,

she knew right away which plant was
responsible.
And which plant would make the
blisters
on my legs stop burning.

EVERYTHING GROWS

April arrives and things
start to bloom.
I look at a picture of my mother
and me.
It was taken just a few months ago.

My hair is longer now.
It has already grown since then.

When I ask if the bad feelings get
smaller,
Dr. Jean-Pierre says that they do not.

But

    she tells me

    life
       gets bigger.

THE WORLD DOESN'T STOP

As unfair as it seems,
life just keeps going.

My peers at school go about
their days unphased. Unchanged.

Wave to me as if I haven't lost
such a big part of myself.

AND THE SEASONS KEEP GOING

like they always have.

Without patience or sympathy
for mourning.

I have no plan for next year
and nothing to look forward to.

GRIEF PARTY

Dr. Jean-Pierre refers me to a
support group

for kids like me
(with parents who live fast—or did).

She says that being with them
might help the loneliness of grief.

I've never talked to anyone
my own age about my mom.

I first join the group
one sunny afternoon in May.

We sit in a circle with a fan
plugged in nearby.

I'm sure that I am sweating
through my sleeves.

I INTRODUCE MYSELF

Hi, um ... my name is Alex.
My mom is—was—an addict.
But uh, not anymore.
Because she's dead now.

My cheeks get hot.
I look down, feeling
embarrassed and awkward.

A girl with a slouchy hat
and dry smile
looks my way and says:

> *Welcome to the club.*
> *You're one of us.*

I ENJOY THE SUPPORT

The group is far better
than I expected.

I laugh when Ella—
     an aspiring comedian—
jokes about how her father has started
collecting coins ever since he stopped
getting high.

I cry when Dennis—
     who likes to be called Boulder—
recalls a familiar-sounding argument
he had with his drunk mother
the night before.

I collect stories as the weeks pass.
I think about telling them to my mom,
even though they're supposed to be
secret.

My partner in crime.

WHAT A STORY

I tell the group about my grief
but also, my dreams.

I show them my camera.
Tell them about the mini-doc
I was supposed to make.

*I don't have enough footage
to make a movie of my mom
even if I wanted to,*
I say, sadly.

> *You could always make
> a movie about us,*
> Ella shrugs.

And I think to myself—
    what a story that could be.

GRADUATION

I decorate my graduation cap with
purple-and-white flowers because

in my favorite picture of my
mother,
she has purple-and-white flowers
in her hair.

I hope that she can see this small
tribute, wherever she is now.

I hope she's watching as I walk
across that stage to get my
diploma.

I hope she watches everywhere I go
in this big, wide world.

HIGH GEAR

My friends from my support group
help re-inspire me.

After graduation,
I kick things into high gear.

I ask if anyone would feel
comfortable being in a short film
about the struggles and strengths
of children with substance-addicted
parents.

To my surprise, many of my new
friends
leap up excitedly.

They jump at the chance to tell
their stories
in their own words.

I've always dreamed of being
a director,
but I never felt this way before.

I am honored to help bring this joy,
this sense of being seen,

to these people,
to my found family.

ALL SUMMER

I work tirelessly
to finish my film.

Ms. Owens cheers me on.
My support group lifts me up.

In October, I'll submit this film
to my top-choice film school.

A film I'm close to.
A film I'm proud of.
A film my mom would love.

My broken heart
swells with pride.

AS ALWAYS

the seasons keep going.

I spend my time with Ella
and the rest of the support group.

And of course, with Mr. and Mrs. S.

They're here for me
as I start my gap year
in the summer.

They're here for me
when I submit my film
in the fall.

They're here for me
when it's been a year
without Mom
in the winter.

And they're here for me
when I get that letter—
the acceptance letter—
in the spring.

CLOSING SCENE

The day I move
to New York City,
Mr. and Mrs. S
drive me to the airport.

I hug them both.

>   *We'll always be here,*
>   says Mr. S.

>   *Our home is always yours,*
>   says Mrs. S.

I promise to call them
all the time.

From my window seat,
as if on cue,
the sun sets.

I can see all the colors in the sky.
Pinks, purples, reds.
Every shade of blue.

I take out my camera
and film it.

I know my mother
would have found it beautiful
in all its chaotic bursts
of color and light—

just as I
remember her.

WANT TO KEEP READING?

If you liked this book, check out another book
from West 44 Books:

SHOOT THE STORM
BY ANNETTE DANIELS TAYLOR

ISBN: 9781978595576

DAD CALLS ME DOUBLE-A

My name is Aaliyah Davis.
Dad says, *Ballers need an alias,*
like a superhero or a rapper.
Double-A, mine.

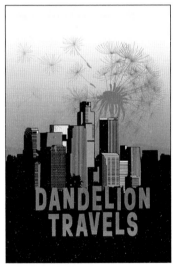

ABOUT THE AUTHOR

Sabine Bradley is a Western New York native, writer, activist, and mother.
She is passionate about the ways human beings relate to each other, and studies Peace and Conflict Theory.
In her spare time she likes to hike and plans on one day walking the entire Empire Trail from Manhattan to Toronto.